The CROCODILES STILL WAIT

FOR EERIK AND IAN, SHAWNA AND SARAH, RALPH
AND STACEY, JACK AND CHRISTOPHER B.

With special thanks to Gus Ben David, Director of the
Felix Neck Wildlife Association, and Dr. Eugene S.
Gaffney, Curator, Department of Vertebrate Paleontol-
ogy, The American Museum of Natural History, for their
help in preparing this book.

Houghton Mifflin/Clarion Books,
52 Vanderbilt Ave., New York, NY 10017

Library of Congress Cataloging in Publication Data
Carrick, Carol.   The Crocodiles Still Wait.
Summary: In prehistoric times, a 50-foot-long mother crocodile
defends her eggs and newly hatched young from attacks by bird
eating dinosaurs and Tyrannosaurus Rex.
1. Crocodiles, Fossil—Juvenile Literature. 2. Dinosauria—Juvenile
Literature. [1. Dinosaurs. 2. Crocodiles, Fossil] I. Carrick, Donald.
II. Title.
QD862.C8C37   568'.14   79-23519   ISBN 0-395-29102-X

The CROCODILES STILL WAIT

BY CAROL CARRICK
PICTURES BY DONALD CARRICK

Houghton Mifflin/Clarion Books/New York

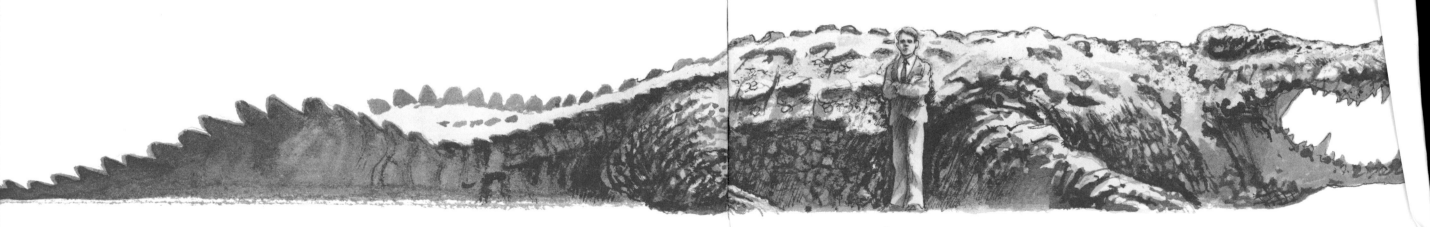

FIFTY-FOOT CROCODILES WITH JAWS SIX FEET LONG HAVE NEVER BEEN SEEN
BY MAN. BUT THEIR BONES HAVE BEEN FOUND. THEY LIVED AT THE TIME OF
THE GREAT DINOSAURS. EXCEPT FOR THEIR SIZE, THEY MUST HAVE BEEN JUST
LIKE THE CROCODILES OF TODAY.

Long before man walked the earth, dinosaurs ruled for a summer that lasted millions of years.

On one of those long ago afternoons a crocodile left the chilly beach to doze in a sun-warmed lake. Like the dinosaurs she was cold-blooded, which meant she could not control her temperature the way warm-blooded animals can. Inside, her body was nearly

the same temperature as the world outside of her, and she had to depend on the sun for heat.

A small herd of duckbilled dinosaurs brought their young to scoop up clams along the shallows. With their shovel-shaped bills they pulled up water plants and poked in the sandy lake bottom.

A pair of bulging eyes and nostrils broke the surface of the lake. The crocodile lunged at the duckbills and seized the leg of a small one. In the confusion as the dinosaurs fled, none of them saw the crocodile drag the young duckbill into deeper water.

While the duckbill struggled for air, the crocodile was breathing calmly through her nostrils which were placed high on the top of her snout. Soon the duckbill stopped thrashing and the water was still again after the crocodile finished her meal.

The next morning the crocodile dragged herself from the cooled water. Horny plates protected the rough skin on her back, and her legs and belly were covered with leathery scales. Dressed in this armor and chain mail, she lay on the beach like a knight on

the battlefield. As she soaked up the warmth from the sun her heart began to beat faster. Blood moved to her stiff muscles, and she felt active again.

A month before, the crocodile and five other females had mated with a big bull crocodile. Soon it would be time for the female crocodiles to lay their eggs.

Since the mating season the bull hissed and bared his teeth whenever another male crocodile entered his territory. The water around him seemed to boil with the bubbles he blew.

A young crocodile slid into the lake. As he swam close, he

foolishly did not honor his father, the big crocodile, by raising his head and showing his throat. This is a crocodile's way of admitting he is weaker.

The old crocodile slapped down his heavy tail, making the upper half of his body shoot up out of the lake. Then the big croc raised great showers of water around himself by noisily bashing his head over and over against the surface of the water.

The younger crocodile tucked his legs and webbed feet against his body, and with powerful strokes of his tail he sped away. But the old bull was in a mean temper. As the female crocodile watched he chased after his son, caught him by the tail, and dragged him to shore.

The bull lumbered back to defend his territory again, leaving the other crocodile to slink off down the beach. This was the last

warning the trespasser would get. Next time he might be killed
and eaten.

On the following day the female dug a shallow pit with her
claws in the sandy soil near the lake. In it she laid forty fragile
white eggs and covered them with earth. During the next week
five other mounds of eggs were laid along the shore by the other
females.

For three months the female crocodile guarded her eggs without eating. During the hottest part of the day she moved to the shade of the undergrowth nearby. But she still watched the nest, growling and snapping her jaws when even her mate passed too close.

One afternoon the temperature rose to 100°, almost a killing

temperature for the cold-blooded crocodiles. The mother was
forced to leave her eggs for an hour's relief in the lake. As she lay
submerged with an anxious eye poking out of the water, a deli-
cate shadow slipped from the forest. It was the dinosaur called
"bird imitator," Ornithomimus, because he must have looked like
an ostrich without feathers.

Ornithomimus lived on insects, fruits, and seeds. Often he was able to snap up small animals, like frogs. But when he was lucky enough to find an unguarded nest full of eggs, he had a feast.

Wasting no time, Ornithomimus began to scratch at the crocodile's nest. If the mother should return, he had no teeth or armor to defend himself. His greatest protection was speed.

When the first eggs were uncovered the dinosaur snatched one
with his long fingers. He was about to break it open when he was
startled by a bellow from the lake. The enraged mother crocodile
rushed out of the water with an amazing burst of speed.

Ornithomimus ran for his life, dropping the egg near the edge
of the clearing. By the time the outraged mother had reached her
broken egg, the dinosaur had disappeared among the trees.

The crocodile wavered between the stolen egg and the uncovered eggs in her nest. Both were unguarded. Many of the
dinosaurs and small mammals were egg eaters. She even had to
watch out for other crocodiles who ate eggs and stray young-
sters.

Then she heard a grunt, and a second grunt, and then a sharp
little bark. It was coming from the cracked egg. The mother
answered softly, "Uh, uh." Then other, muffled grunts came from
the nest behind her.

The broken egg trembled. A window was torn through the soft inner shell and a small snout with a horny egg-cutting tooth on its tip appeared. The struggle inside the egg continued until it was pried apart and a miniature crocodile wriggled free.

The mother scooped the little one up in her mouth and carried him to the nest. It was now swarming with newly hatched crocodiles who soon headed for the lake.

Just before sunset, cries came from the eggs that were still buried. The mother called to them, scratching away the rest of the sand covering.

The old bull crocodile was nowhere in sight. After the eggs began to hatch he lost interest in the females. Now he was resting in a den he had dug out under tree roots farther down the shore. Suddenly the evening quiet was shattered by the bellow of frightened duckbills crashing through the forest. Behind them a

hulking form was hard to make out in the gloom. But there was
no doubt about the brutal head outlined against the sky. It was
Tyrannosaurus Rex.

The first of the duckbills broke into the open. They pounded
across the beach and charged into the water. Like the crocodiles,
the duckbills were excellent swimmers. Once in deep water their
strong tails could sweep them out of the Tyrannosaur's reach.

The five other female crocodiles had scattered, and their nests were trampled under the duckbills' hoofs. But the one mother crocodile stood firm. She squatted over her nest, protecting the last of her hatching babies with her body.

One of the slowest duckbills, running on the edge of the herd, was startled to find his way blocked by jaws even larger than the Tyrannosaur's. The mother crocodile hissed. He swerved to avoid her and stumbled, then scrambled to his feet again.

At last the duckbill plunged into the water, but too much time
had been lost. The Tyrannosaur's claws had hooked into his spine
and his heavy weight carried them both under.

The Tyrannosaur's double-edged teeth sank into the duckbill's neck. The duckbill kicked and thrashed his tail until the jaws of the Tyrannosaur clamped shut.

From her nest the crocodile watched the Tyrannosaur climb out
of the lake. His heavy body was not designed for swimming, and it
took all of his strength to pull himself up from the lake bottom. He
had to leave the duckbill behind.

The crocodile backed away from him but her jaws were stretched wide. She was ready to put up a fight. Her eyes glowed red and her wicked teeth gleamed in the moonlight. The Tyrannosaur stumbled into the wreckage of the forest. He would look for an easier prey.

The mother crocodile gently cracked the unopened eggs with her
teeth to help the last of the babies free. When all the hatchlings
had reached the safety of the lake, she twisted off a joint from the
duckbill carcass. She had not eaten such a meal since her eggs had

been laid. Her babies swarmed around her, snapping at each other. Although she did not feed them, the mother crocodile allowed them to eat the scraps.

DINOSAURS DISAPPEARED 60 MILLION YEARS AGO AFTER DOMINATING THE
EARTH FOR 120 MILLION YEARS, BUT THE CROCODILES REMAINED. ONE MILLION
YEARS AGO HUMANS BEGAN TO RULE THE EARTH. SOME FEARED AND WOR-
SHIPED CROCODILES AS GODS. OTHERS HUNTED THEM DOWN. BUT IN WARM
LAKES AND WATERWAYS, THE CROCODILES STILL WAIT.

ABCDEFGHIJ—RA—876543210/80